Mouse

Owl

Rabbit

For Jensen and Sebastian
LM

First published 2018 by Macmillan Children's Books
an imprint of Pan Macmillan
20 New Wharf Road, London N1 9RR
Associated companies throughout the world
www.panmacmillan.com

ISBN 978-1-5098-2845-6

1 3 5 7 9 8 6 4 2

A CIP catalogue record for this book is available
from the British Library.

Printed in China

Frog Hops Off!

MACMILLAN CHILDREN'S BOOKS

Frog was always very bouncy.
But today he was feeling very bouncy indeed!
He couldn't wait to get to Twit Twoo School.
His teacher, Miss Hoot, had said that today
they were going . . . exploring!

Frog didn't want to hold Daddy's hand. He was off!

When Daddy finally managed to catch up with Frog he said,
"Now listen to what Miss Hoot says today.
No bouncing off on your own."

"Yes Daddy," said Frog,
who was trying to hold
in a huge hop.

Frog got to school very early.
Eventually the other children arrived.

They were all very excited, and the first thing they explored was each other's lunchboxes.

Frog managed to drop his on the floor. Mole helped him pick it up.

Owl was very proud of his lunch. He had made it all himself.

Rabbit had already eaten most of hers.

Miss Hoot gathered the class around.
"Today, children," she said, "we are going underground."

Frog jumped up, knocking over his lunchbox again.
It was going to be even better than he'd thought!

"Now listen carefully," continued Miss Hoot, talking to the class but looking at Frog. "Hold hands with your partner, and no running off. I don't want anyone getting lost."

Miss Hoot said Frog could be her partner.
They set off with Miss Hoot and Frog leading the way.
Soon they came to a big, dark hole. Down they went.

Frog could hardly control his bounces. It was all so exciting! He'd never been underground before.

He wanted to jump off ahead to see
what was around the next corner,
but he remembered what Daddy
and Miss Hoot had said and he
was really trying to be good.

Mouse held on tight to Rabbit's hand. She was feeling a little bit nervous.

Rabbit wondered if it was lunchtime yet.

Mole found a worm. So did Owl. It was the same worm.

Frog thought worms were boring. He was much more interested in what was up ahead. He was a brave explorer after all.

Frog hopped around the corner. "I won't go far," he thought to himself. There was a bend in the tunnel. "I'll just see what's down here," said Frog.

He hopped round the bend, and then around another . . . and then another.

As Frog hopped further
down the tunnel, he
started to wonder.

What if someone lives down here?
Not a worm, but someone not very nice.
A goblin. A troll. A dragon!

Frog stopped hopping.
He didn't feel quite so brave now.
He thought he'd explored enough.

But which way was back?
Uh oh! Frog was lost!

He sat down and began to cry.
"Oh why didn't I listen to Miss Hoot?" he
sobbed. "Now I'll be lost forever, and I'll have
to live with the goblins and the trolls and the
dragons, and I'll never see my daddy again!"

And with that, Frog really wailed.

Suddenly Frog stopped sobbing. What was that he'd heard?
Something was coming down the tunnel!
"A dragon!" cried Frog.

And by the sound of the footsteps, it wasn't just a dragon.
It was some goblins and trolls too!

Frog closed his eyes tight. He was doomed!

But . . .

"There you are!" said the
dragon in a kindly voice.
A voice that actually sounded
a lot like Miss Hoot.

Frog opened his eyes . . .

It *was* Miss Hoot, and all the other children!
Not a dragon or trolls or goblins at all.
"Didn't I tell you not to bounce off ahead?" said Miss Hoot.
"You must learn to listen, Frog."

"Yes Miss Hoot. I'm really sorry Miss Hoot," said Frog in a relieved voice. He was feeling a little bit silly now. "I won't do it again. I'll be a really good listener!"

"I'm happy to hear that," said Miss Hoot. "Now, who'd like lunch?" And all the animals cheered.

Miss Hoot led the class back through the
tunnels and out into the sunshine.

When they reached the picnic spot, she said she had
a special treat for the children. Frog was still being
a good listener, and he heard that very clearly!

Frog was worried that he wouldn't be able to have a treat as he'd been a bit naughty, but Miss Hoot said he could.

He was so pleased that he nearly started bouncing again, but he managed to control himself.

After a lovely lunch and a bit of a play, it was
time to go home. Here was Daddy.

Frog was so pleased that he bounced his biggest
bounce of the day! He just couldn't help himself.

Frog and Daddy hopped off together, and this time Frog held his daddy's hand all the way home!

Miss Hoot

Mole

Frog

Mouse

Owl

Rabbit